TONY JEFFERSON IN

Beyond a Doubt

Agnes M. Hagen

New Readers Press

For Roy who gave me a great idea.

Beyond a Doubt
ISBN 1-56420-278-X
Copyright © 2001
New Readers Press
U.S. Publishing Division of Laubach Literacy
1320 Jamesville Avenue, Syracuse, New York 13210

All rights reserved. No part of this book may be reproduced or transmitted in any form or by any means, electronic or mechanical, including photocopying, recording, or by any information storage and retrieval system, without permission in writing from the publisher.

Printed in the United States of America
9 8 7 6 5 4 3 2 1

Director of Acquisitions and Development: Christina Jagger
Content Editor: Terrie Lipke
Copy Editor: Judi Lauber
Production Director: Heather Witt
Designer: Kimbrly Koennecke
Cover Designer: Kimbrly Koennecke
Cover Illustrator: James P. Wallace
Production Specialist: Alexander Jones

All proceeds from the sale of New Readers Press materials support literacy programs in the United States and worldwide.

Chapter 1

I looked up from my desk when my office doorbell jingled. The man who walked in was tall and well dressed. What struck me most about him, however, was the serious look on his face. This man was on a mission.

"Can I help you?" I offered.

"I hope so," he replied. He propped his leather briefcase on the floor next to my desk. Then he reached across to shake my hand. "My name is Ted Hayes. I'm a lawyer from Richmond.

Harry Lyman is my brother-in-law. He's the one who told me that you're the best private detective in town."

I smiled and nodded. I was the only private eye in the small town of Stanton, Virginia. Still, it was nice to know that a local police officer was recommending me.

I was new at this business. Until a year ago, I'd been a Baltimore cop. Then my partner was gunned down in front of me. I just couldn't get the shooting off my mind. I needed to take a break from police work. So I left the only job I'd ever had.

My dog, Chance, and I headed south to Virginia. We stayed with my grandparents in Bath County. While I was there, I got involved with a missing person case. It made me realize that there were some aspects of police work I still enjoyed. I moved into the nearby town of Stanton and opened my own detective agency.

Ted Hayes sat down and pulled the briefcase onto his lap. He opened it and removed a folder and some photographs. He placed them on my desk.

"I'm here because of a man who's doing time at Stanton Prison," he began. "I hope that you can help me prove he's innocent."

"What's the crime?" I asked.

"Murder," he said flatly.

Images of murder cases I had worked on in Baltimore flashed through my mind. I pictured my partner lying in his own blood. I thought of his wife and children waiting for him to return home from work. I thought of all the good and bad times we'd had together. This would be the first murder case I would work on in over a year. I wondered if I was ready for this. I could turn it down. There were other detectives between here and Richmond.

The lawyer's voice shook me back to the present. "Is anything wrong?" he asked.

"No," I replied as firmly as I could. "What makes you so sure this guy is innocent?"

Ted Hayes smiled confidently. "Mr. Jefferson," he began.

"Call me Tony," I said.

"This man, Ernie Clement, was found guilty with very little evidence. He's a drunk, but he's not a killer. His public defender was fresh out of law school.

"Ernie was sure he'd be free in no time. But the trial didn't go his way. When it was over, he was sentenced to 20 years."

I reached over and picked up the photographs. They were pictures of a murder scene. I thumbed through them while Ted continued.

"As soon as he could, Ernie went to the prison law library for help. One of the aides there helped him set up an appeal. He also talked to the prison chaplain who contacted me. When I heard his story, I agreed to take the case for free.

"Tony, I've spoken to Ernie, and I believe he is innocent. If I'm right, then the killer is still free. I hope that bothers you as much as it bothers me."

Chapter 2

"I remember reading about the sentencing in the newspaper," I said. "But the murder must have happened before I moved here. Tell me about it."

I poured Ted a cup of coffee, and he settled back in his chair. "It was almost two years ago. A local man named Ben Jones was found dead out near Beaver Creek. He had been hit on the back of the head with a blunt object. The murder weapon was never found. It was a rainy night, so some evidence may have washed away. One thing the police did find was a wallet—Ernie Clement's wallet. It was found a few yards away from the body. The police believe Ernie dropped it as he fled the crime scene."

"Do you think it was a setup?" I asked.

"Maybe," Ted replied. "Ernie can't explain how his wallet got there. He told me he'd spent the evening at the bar in the Robin's Nest Restaurant. He got drunk and walked home in the rain. The next thing he remembers is the police pounding on his door. He also told me he recalled seeing the Bluebirds at the restaurant. The Bluebirds—"

"I know," I said proudly. "It's a women's softball team." "My friend, Julie Simon, plays first base."

Ted nodded. "Yeah, they won the season championship that evening. The owner of the Robin's Nest is their sponsor. He invited the team back to the restaurant after the game to celebrate. The fact that Ernie remembers seeing the girls didn't give him an alibi. The coroner said Jones was murdered between 8 P.M. and 10 P.M.—after the team arrived. And Beaver Creek's just on the west edge of town. He would have had plenty of time to get there."

I got up to get a cup of coffee, and I refilled Ted's cup.

"There was a large crowd at the restaurant that night," Ted continued. "The bartenders and waitresses were very busy. A couple of them remembered seeing Ernie, but no one is sure what time he left.

"At the trial, several people testified that Ernie and Jones didn't get along. In fact, they had quite a fight just a week before the murder. It happened in the main aisle of the local hardware store. Ernie had been drinking, of course, and he bumped into Jones. They argued about Lee Ruiz. She's a waitress over at Sammy's Diner. Ernie took a swing at Ben, and the two of them went at it. Jones knocked Ernie to the floor before anyone could break them up."

"So Ernie admits that he and Jones were less than friendly?" I asked Ted.

"Ernie hated Jones," Ted replied. "It was all because of Lee Ruiz. Ernie's had a crush on her for a long time. She wouldn't date him because of his drinking, but they became friends.

"When Lee started seeing Jones, Ernie tried to break them up. That made Jones mad. And I guess he had a habit of taking his anger out on Lee. Ernie said she tried to hide the bruises and black eyes from him, but he figured out what was going on. And that's when things heated up between Ernie and Jones."

"If Jones was such a hothead," I said

to Ted, "there must have been other folks who didn't like him. Were there any other suspects?"

Ted sounded very sure that Ernie was not guilty. "Not at the time, Tony. I don't know who killed Jones. But I wouldn't be here unless I believed Ernie Clement is innocent. And I'm hoping you will be able to track down the real killer." He was so confident that I couldn't help believing him.

"Give me what you have on this case, and I'll get on it right away," I said. I got up from my desk to walk Ted out.

Ted pointed to the folder and photos on my desk. "These are the photos the police took at the murder scene. In the folder, you'll find names and addresses of some of the people involved. I will get you the trial transcripts, too. I'd like you to get started right away on this," he said. "Get background checks on everybody involved. And find out what you can about Frank Hudson. He and Jones were in business together. Maybe Hudson had a bigger role in this than the police suspected." His voice had an air of authority.

"You've got it," I replied.

Chapter 3

My first stop was the city library. I read last year's newspaper articles on the Ben Jones murder. I found out that Jones and his partner, Frank Hudson, owned some shabby rental properties. In the article I read, their tenants complained about the apartments being in disrepair. There were problems with the electrical wiring that made the lights go out frequently. And the plumbing was in bad enough shape to be considered a health hazard.

During Ernie's trial, the IRS investigated Frank Hudson for tax fraud. It found that Frank and Jones were cheating on their taxes to get big refunds. The two men deducted thousands of dollars that they claimed to be spending on repairs. Now Frank was doing time at Stanton Prison, too.

The newspaper even printed interviews with some of the tenants. One of the tenants, Jason Brown, was a guard at Stanton Prison. Jones was threatening to evict Brown and his family. Brown had a pregnant wife and a 5-year-old son at the time. He had withheld one month's rent to force Jones to make some repairs to the apartment.

When Brown showed up at the rental office to try and work out an agreement, Jones started a fight. He pushed Brown and threatened to change the locks on the apartment. Ben Jones had more enemies than friends.

Beyond a Doubt

I was ready for a break, so I stopped for a late lunch at Sammy's Diner. The counter waitress was a slender, brown-haired woman. She would have been pretty, but her mouth was set in a permanent frown. It looked like life had beaten the joy out of her.

I noticed her name tag as she delivered my beef stew. It said "Lee." Was this the woman Ernie had fought with Ben about? I watched her as she worked. She was capable and quick, but she never cracked a smile. I felt sorry for her, and I left her a generous tip.

My next stop was the police station. I found Harry buried behind a pile of paperwork. "Tony," he wheezed. "What are you doing here?"

"Does the name Ted Hayes ring a bell?" I asked.

"Humph," replied Harry as he sipped coffee from a paper cup. "He's my brother-in-law. He's a big-shot lawyer over in Richmond. What's he up to?"

"He came to see me this morning about the Ben Jones murder."

"Oh yeah," Harry said. "He was talking about that last weekend when we got together. He's really serious about proving Ernie didn't do it. Tell you the truth, I've had some doubts myself. Ernie's a drunk and a troublemaker, but I never would have pegged him for a murderer."

"So you'll help me with this?" I asked.

"I'm due in court in a couple of minutes," Harry grunted, pushing a battered file toward me.

"You had it ready! You knew I was coming," I exclaimed.

"Leave it on my desk when you're through," Harry said with a wink. He swallowed the last of his coffee and shuffled out the door.

Beyond a Doubt

Chapter 4

Ted Hayes arranged for me to visit Ernie Clement. So the next day, I made my way to Stanton Prison for a chat with the convicted killer.

A tall chain-link fence topped with coils of razor wire surrounded the prison. On the way in, I was asked to raise my arms while a guard patted me down. Then I was sent through a metal detector. I was led toward the visiting area. Ted had hired me as part of Ernie's defense team, so we were allowed to talk in private.

A guard brought me to a small room with no windows. There was a table with two chairs in the center of the room. A tall skinny guy sat stiffly in one chair and stared at the wall. He was only 32, but the look on his face reminded me of that waitress at Sammy's.

This was the guy I was supposed to help? He looked like he'd already given up. I sat across from him and introduced myself. He smiled a little when I mentioned Ted Hayes.

Ernie brushed a strand of dark hair off his face and began to speak. "One of the guys down in the law library told me I could get help," he began with a slow drawl. "I didn't know what to do. I . . . I didn't kill him! I know everybody thinks that I'm just saying that, but I swear I never killed anyone."

"Help me then," I said firmly. "Give me something to go on. Your wallet was found at the scene, and you don't have an alibi. Why should I believe you?"

"Because I wouldn't do a thing like that," he said with confidence.

"That wasn't reason enough for the jury to believe you," I pointed out.

He looked around the room and nodded. "OK, so I can't remember what happened at the bar after that girls' softball team arrived," he said. "I know I couldn't find my jacket when the cops came to get me. And my clothes were still damp. So I must have walked home in the rain without it. It's not all that unusual for me to get so drunk that I don't remember how I got home.

"When I got to the police station, I realized I didn't have my wallet, either. I just figured I left it in my jacket pocket."

"Did you ever find your jacket?" I asked.

"No," Ernie replied.

"What about the fight with Ben Jones at the hardware store?" I asked. "There were witnesses who said you threatened to kill him."

"You don't know how he was treating Lee. She tried to hide it, but he'd beaten her nearly to death more than once. And she's my best friend. When everybody else gave up on me, Lee tried to help me clean up my act. She still hasn't given up on me. She's been writing me letters since they put me here. I owe that lady big time."

"What was she doing with a guy like Jones?" I asked.

"She's such a kind person," he answered. "Lee tries to see the good in everybody. She thought Jones could change. Whenever I saw her with a black eye or a bruise, she'd say he didn't mean it. I think he even convinced her that it was her own fault. She deserves so much better. When I get out of here, I'm going to take care of her." He sat up straight and said it again. "I am going to get out of this place. And I'm going to take good care of Lee."

Finally, I could see a glimmer of hope in Ernie's eyes. Maybe he was a fighter after all.

Chapter 5

Julie invited me to her house for dinner that evening. We've been good friends ever since I came to this area. My grandmother introduced me to Julie and her mother shortly after I arrived. Julie's sister, Dawn, had been missing, and Mamaw asked me to help find her.

I guess you could say that was my first case as a private detective. And Julie's common-sense advice was very helpful to me. I've grown to trust and rely on Julie. Sometimes, just by discussing a case with her, she can get me to see the facts in a new light. I couldn't wait to talk to her about Ernie Clement.

Julie had no trouble remembering the evening the Bluebirds won the championship. The game had been so exciting. Also one of her teammates, Kim Edwards, had had her tote bag stolen that night.

"We searched all over the restaurant," Julie said. "We even looked in the car, but we never found it. Kim told the police about it the next day. There was nothing valuable in it, so she wasn't too upset.

"That's all I recall about that night. Well, that and the celebrating! The game went into an extra inning. We won just as it was starting to rain. Then the folks at the Robin's Nest kept bringing out free pizzas and pitchers of beer. We had a great night."

I smiled, remembering how thrilled she'd been when she first told me about her winning team. "Tomorrow morning, I'm going to Beaver Creek to check out the crime scene," I said. "Want to tag along?"

"Gee, Beaver Creek is full of trout," Julie giggled. "Should I bring my fishing rod?"

"We'll be fishing for clues, not trout," I said with a laugh.

* * *

The following morning was warm and sunny. Chance and I climbed into my aging car and headed for Beaver Creek. Julie was already there, waiting for me.

"What can I do to help?" she asked eagerly.

I took out the photos of the crime scene and showed them to her. By matching up some landmarks, we located the area where the body was found.

"I'm going to use the metal detector to see if I can find anything unusual in this area. It was stormy the night of the murder, so some evidence could have been washed into the creek or buried in the sand. And now that almost two years have passed, I'm not sure we'll find anything at all."

Julie followed Chance along the shoreline while I used the metal detector to sweep the area. Chance was retired from the police force, too. He was trained at a police canine academy, and he still had a great nose.

I pulled my metal detector out of the car trunk and began to search the crime scene. I wasn't sure I'd find anything but empty soda cans and bottle caps. But for some reason, I believed Ernie was innocent. So I had to try my best.

Julie was following Chance, watching him sniff the wet sand. Suddenly, he stopped to dig. "Tony!" she hollered. "Chance found something!"

I turned and ran toward them. As I approached, Chance lifted his head to look at me. Then he picked something up in his mouth.

"Julie," I said, "It's a pair of sunglasses." I held out my hand, and Chance dropped the glasses in it. They had bright red frames, and the gold initials *KE* were on the bottom of one lens.

"Those look like Kim's!" Julie exclaimed. "They were in her tote bag. How did they get here?"

"I don't know," I said. "But I'm going to find out." I carefully slipped the glasses into a plastic bag.

Then we continued to search the shoreline. Chance spent a long time sniffing a large hunk of driftwood that had washed up onto the shore. So I asked Julie to wrap it in plastic and put it in the trunk. My metal detector was turning up mostly coins and trash. But I did dig up a metal flashlight. It

Beyond a Doubt

looked very old and rusty, but I bagged it up to take to the lab.

Chapter 6

Julie called Kim Edwards from her car phone and asked her to meet us at the police station. We were showing Harry the items we'd found by the creek when Kim walked in.

"Those are my glasses!" Kim said right away. "Julie told me they were at Beaver Creek. How did they end up there?"

"That's what I'm going to try to figure out," I replied.

"You told me that your sunglasses

were in your tote bag the night of the big game," Julie said to Kim. "What else was in the bag when it disappeared?"

"Not much," Kim said. "Just my hat, an umbrella, and a water bottle, I think."

"We didn't find those things," said Julie.

"Harry will need to take your fingerprints," I told Kim. "That way we can tell if anyone else touched your sunglasses."

Harry agreed to send the glasses to the lab in Richmond right away. "I'll also have the flashlight and the driftwood checked for blood and prints," he said. "I guess the killer could have used that piece of wood to hit Jones before he tossed it into the creek. It would take a while before it washed up on shore again."

Late that evening, I was in my office when the phone rang. Harry had some news. "We lifted a couple of prints off those sunglasses you found," he reported. "So I ran them through the computer."

"Did you get a match?" I asked.

"Yes," Harry said hesitantly. "But I'm not sure what it means. Kim's prints showed up, of course, and also Rhonda Hudson's."

"Rhonda Hudson? Is that Frank's wife?" I asked. "Does she have a criminal record?"

"Yeah," Harry replied. "I've had her in here a few times on shoplifting and petty theft. She and Frank are peas in a pod. Neither one of 'em has ever done an honest day's work."

"Why don't you talk to her?" I suggested. "You've questioned her before. Maybe you can find out what she was doing with Kim's glasses."

"And how did the glasses end up near the murder scene?" Harry pondered. "I'll let you know how it goes with her. No word yet on the flashlight and the wood—maybe in a day or two."

"Thanks, Harry," I said. "I couldn't do this without you."

After I hung up the phone, I couldn't stop thinking about Frank and Rhonda Hudson. Ted Hayes was right about Frank's dirty business dealings. I had learned that Frank had been fired from a company in Richmond a few years back. They suspected him of padding his expense accounts as well as stealing company property. I guess they didn't have enough evidence to bring charges, so they just got rid of him.

Now I was starting to think that maybe Frank and Rhonda were a team. All along, the police were only looking for one killer. What if there were two?

From what Harry said, Frank didn't complain too much when he got sent to prison. Heck, a couple of years for tax fraud sure beats doing life for murder.

Chapter 7

I woke up hungry the next morning. So I decided to go to Sammy's for a stack of buckwheat pancakes. As luck would have it, Lee waited on me at the counter. Her face was set in the same gloomy frown as before. When she poured my coffee, I introduced myself.

"My name's Tony Jefferson," I said. "You're Lee Ruiz, right?"

"Yeah, that's right," she responded. "Do I know you?"

"I recently met a friend of yours," I

said. "Ernie Clement."

"Really?" she asked. She almost smiled, and I saw the lines on her face soften a little. "How's he doing?"

Lee stepped over to the cash register to ring up a customer. Then she refilled my coffee.

"As well as can be expected," I replied. "I'm trying to help Ernie's lawyer get him out of prison. I was hoping you could tell me about Ben Jones."

Lee sighed deeply and shook her head like she was trying to forget something. "I still can't believe I let myself get involved with him," she said. "He used to come in here to bring me flowers and sweet-talk me. We had a good time at first. He seemed like a nice guy. By the time he started beating on me, I really thought I was in love with him."

The diner was nearly empty now that the breakfast rush was over. Lee sat down and lit a cigarette. "I tried to hide what was happening," she said. "But Ernie figured it out. He kept nagging me to break up with Ben. I was afraid of what Ben would do if I stopped seeing him. He threatened to kill me—and Ernie."

Lee gritted her teeth and watched the cigarette smoke swirl. "I'm not sorry that he's dead," she admitted. "It was a relief, actually. But I know Ernie didn't do it. He wouldn't lie to me about a thing like that. He's told me more than once that he wished he had the nerve to kill Ben. There were times when I prayed for the same nerve."

On the way back to my office, I kept thinking about what Lee had said. I've met a lot of criminals and killers in my line of work, and Lee didn't seem like either. I had a hunch that I had not met the person who killed Ben Jones—yet.

When I returned to my office, the answering machine was blinking. I was glad to hear Harry's voice on the tape. He said he had spoken with Rhonda Hudson, so I hurried down to the station.

"Harry!" I said, rushing to his desk. "What's up?"

"I thought you'd want to know I questioned Mrs. Hudson about those sunglasses. You'll be interested to hear the story she told. She's still here, waiting to sign a statement. Come on. I told her you'd want to talk to her."

Harry led me to a desk where a young female officer was entering information on a computer. Another woman sat opposite her. So this was Rhonda Hudson. She was pale and thin, and she twisted her wedding ring nervously while she talked.

Harry was right. Rhonda told quite a story. She was terrified that someday the cops would find out she'd been at Beaver Creek the night of the murder. So when Harry said he had fingerprints that placed her at the crime scene, she told him everything.

Rhonda confessed to having been at the creek that night. She said that she and Frank had been arguing. She needed to get out of the house, so she went to the Robin's Nest to have a drink. When the Bluebirds arrived, it got real crowded and noisy. Rhonda saw a chance to steal some quick cash. And with Frank under investigation for fraud, they needed money badly.

Rhonda said she saw Ernie put his wallet in his coat pocket. Then he left the coat on a table while he went to the bar. She figured he was drunk enough not to remember his coat. She grabbed it and headed for the door. On the way out, she snatched a tote bag that was hanging on the back of a chair.

"I wanted to get out of there before anyone saw me," she said. "So I ran to the car. I drove straight home. The creek is out behind my apartment building. It was dark and raining, and no one was around. I walked along the creek, and picked the money out of Ernie's wallet. Then I just tossed the wallet on the ground. I must have dropped the sunglasses when I was digging through the tote bag.

"All of a sudden, I heard voices—two men, I think. It sounded like they were coming toward me. So I ran. It was raining hard, so I put the jacket on. And I tossed the tote bag in the dumpster by the parking lot. I didn't see anyone. I just ran."

"Well, Harry," I said, "That explains why Ernie's wallet was found near the body. But it still doesn't tell us who the killer is."

"Haven't I told you that it takes patience to catch a criminal?" Harry chuckled.

Chapter 8

I was still at the police station when my cell phone rang. It was Ernie. He sounded breathless and panic-stricken.

"You've got to get me out of here, Tony," he pleaded. "He's going to kill me!"

"Who's going to kill you?" I demanded.

"Whoever left me this note," he said. "It must be someone inside the prison. What am I going to do?"

Beyond a Doubt

I didn't get a chance to tell him the good news about his wallet. All I said was, "I'll get there as soon as I can." And then the line went dead.

Back in my office, I dialed Ted's number in Richmond. "Ted," I began, "It's Tony. Harry says you're good friends with the warden at Stanton Prison."

"Uh-oh," Ted replied. "I'm afraid to ask what you're thinking."

I told Ted about Rhonda Hudson's confession and the call from Ernie. "I've talked to everyone involved except Frank Hudson," I said. "Maybe from inside the prison, I can check out Frank's story. I may be able to find out if Frank has been talking about the murder. Some criminals like to brag. And while I'm there, I can speak to that guard, Jason Brown. He knew firsthand what a swindler Ben Jones was. I'd like to know if they worked out their differences before Jones died.

"Besides, if Ernie's right, someone inside doesn't want us to know who the killer is. Ernie could be in danger. This way, I can help protect him.

"All right," Ted said, "I'll do it—to protect Ernie. I'll talk to the warden right away. But Tony, who's going to protect you?"

"Don't worry about me," I said. "I'm still a cop at heart. I'm used to taking care of myself."

Barely an hour went by before Ted called back. He talked to the warden, who had a guard go and check on Ernie. He was safe for now. The warden agreed to give me three days in the prison. He said he'd put me in to replace a guard who'd asked for some time off.

Ted told me to report to Stanton Prison at 5 A.M. to be fitted for a uniform. He also said the warden recommended I get my hair cut military style, to help me blend in.

Only the warden and assistant warden would know my real identity. Even the shift commander was told only that I was transferred from a prison on the other side of the state.

The prison rules were faxed to me, and I spent the evening studying them. I was assigned to the floor where Jason Brown was in charge. Ernie Clement and Frank Hudson were both on that floor.

I called Julie and asked her to take care of Chance for me. I'd be working long shifts at the prison, and Chance isn't used to being alone. Julie came right over to pick up Chance. She told me she was worried about me and asked me to be careful.

The next morning, it felt natural to be back in uniform. My first job was to help Jason assemble the men for morning count. The whistle blew, and I headed to my floor.

The inmates had already begun

lining up along the wall. Jason was shaking a few sleepyheads awake. He motioned for me to check the beds at my end of the hall. Ernie Clement was still snoring in his cell. I wondered if he would recognize me, with my newly shorn hair. Leaning over him, I yelled, "Get up!" Then I looked him in the eyes and whispered, "You don't know me!"

Ernie gasped. Then he smiled as he pulled on his robe and headed for the wall.

For the rest of the morning, I had to supervise the inmates who were on cleaning duty. I got to walk around and check the place out. Four men occupied each cell. There wasn't much room for privacy. I checked the bed chart in the guard office. Frank Hudson shared a prized corner cell, far from the noisy recreational center.

Chapter 9

I met Frank Hudson when he showed up at the guard office to get a library pass. Unlike most of the other inmates, he actually seemed concerned with his appearance. He was clean shaven and his shirt was tucked in. His prison-issue boots were polished to a high shine.

I tried to strike up a conversation with him. "So, Frank, who's your favorite author?" I asked.

"Oh, I'm not reading for pleasure

right now. I'm doing research for a book I'm writing," Frank replied. The smug smile on his face told me that he thought he was smarter than the average criminal.

"That sounds interesting," I said, hinting for further information. But Frank just smiled and hurried off to the library.

Jason Brown came up behind me. "You know, he's a tutor at the school here," Jason said. He pointed down the hallway toward Frank. "Teacher says he's great with students preparing to take the GED exam. A lot of the guys here don't have high school diplomas. Studying for the GED gives them something worthwhile to do. I think that book he's writing is some kind of history text for GED students. Some of these crooks will be able to get real jobs when they get out of here."

"Speaking of jobs," I said, "I heard that you have more than one. Is that true?"

"Yeah," Jason replied as he sipped a soda. "I work part-time downtown as a security guard. My wife quit her job a year and a half ago when our daughter was born. The baby was premature and had some problems. My wife just couldn't stand the thought of leaving her in day care. I have a son, too. He's almost 7."

"Working two jobs, you must not spend much time with your family," I said.

"Yeah, but it'll be worth it in the end," he replied. "We've been in this run-down apartment, and it's no place to raise kids. I tried to get the landlord to make repairs, but that didn't happen. So we're trying to save up for a down payment for a house. I want my kids to grow up in a nice place."

"That's a tough break," I said. "Your landlord sounds like a jerk."

"He was," Jason told me, "but he's dead now. As a matter of fact, Frank Hudson was the guy's partner. But he's in no position to help now. So the city inspector ordered some repairs made to bring the building up to code."

"You must know Frank pretty well then. What's he like?" I asked.

"Ah, he's harmless," said Jason. "He was the brains on the team, and Jones was the brawn. It was Frank who devised the tax-fraud scheme. He actually brags about it. I've heard him giving tips on how to cheat the IRS. Some people never learn."

"So Ben Jones was your landlord?" I asked Jason. "I read about his murder in the newspaper. And here you are guarding the guy who killed him, Ernie Clement."

"Yeah, isn't that a kick? Some folks actually believe Ernie didn't do it, but not me," Jason said. "He's just the kind of weasel you would never suspect had the nerve. But I think anyone is capable of murder if he's forced into an impossible situation.

"You can't tell the guilty from the innocent just by looking. You'd never guess Frank Hudson was a crook if you didn't see him behind bars!"

As my 12-hour shift dragged on, I found myself assigned to the chow hall. I was covering for another guard who'd gone on supper break. As I sat at the raised desk overlooking the dining hall, I watched the prisoners with interest. Who were the murderers among them? While I kept watch over the men, I thought about who could have killed Ben Jones.

First of all, there was Ernie Clement. He was angry with Jones for mistreating Lee. But was he angry enough to kill a man in cold blood?

Then there was Frank Hudson, Jones' partner in crime. Did he kill Ben in an attempt to cover up the tax-fraud scheme? Maybe the men argued about splitting profits. Or maybe Jones resisted going along with Hudson's plan.

Jason Brown was mad at Jones for trying to throw his family out on the street. But is that motive to kill someone? He didn't look like a killer to me.

My thoughts wandered outside the prison walls. Even Lee Ruiz had reason to strike out at Jones. She could have finally decided to fight back after all the beatings.

And what about Rhonda Hudson? How much did she really know about her husband's plan? Maybe she saw Jones as a threat. She had already admitted to being at the scene of the murder.

My first day at the prison was nearly over, and I was no closer to finding the truth. Jason was right. You can't tell the murderers by the clothes they wear.

Chapter 10

I couldn't believe how tired I felt when my alarm rang the next morning. I was glad not to worry about walking Chance. With only two days left at Stanton Prison, I'd have to make the most of my time. Somehow, I had to stir things up to see if I could get Frank to start talking about Ben Jones. My mind raced as I considered what I might say that would trigger a reaction from the real killer. Of course, if Jones' killer wasn't inside the prison, I might get no reaction at all.

My second day at Stanton Prison was much like the one before. I supervised inmates who worked in my area. I issued passes for inmates to go to the library, recreational center, and weight room. I spent some time talking to Jason. He was calm and levelheaded. He did not seem like the type who would bash a man's skull.

I finally thought of a plan to stir up the pot a bit. I called Ted and asked him to visit Ernie. When Ted Hayes arrived, Ernie was paged. All the men on his floor knew he was going to see his lawyer.

Ted told Ernie to pretend that we had a lead on the murderer. He told him to act like it would all be over soon. And he asked Ernie to be careful not to blow my cover.

At supper, I overheard Ernie telling his cell mates that he would be getting released. I didn't think it would be long before the news spread. Sure enough, by lights-out, everyone was whispering about Ernie Clement.

* * *

My third day at the prison started like the other two. I went to Ernie's bunk to wake him for morning count, but this time he was waiting for me. He slipped me a note he found when he woke up. One line was typed neatly on a sheet of notebook paper.

MURDERER COMMITS SUICIDE IN HIS CELL.

I folded the note and put it in my pocket. "Ernie," I said quietly, "You shouldn't go anywhere alone today. Stick with a group of guys. If anything suspicious happens, make lots of noise to get the guards' attention."

As soon as I could, I called Harry. He said he'd dust the note for prints. I put it in an envelope and left it for him at the warden's office.

Chapter 11

During breakfast, I paced from table to table, trying to listen in on what the men were talking about. Nothing unusual was going on. I paid careful attention to Frank's table. He was bragging about his letter-writing skills. He offered to write letters for the other men in exchange for money or cigarettes. I wondered if he would type the letters on notebook paper.

Jason wasn't in a very talkative mood. He kept to himself most of the day. So when I got a chance, I slipped away to visit the library. One of the inmate aides greeted me right away. He was an elderly man with gray hair who seemed to enjoy his work.

"What can I do for you, sir?" he asked cheerfully.

"I was wondering if you had a typewriter in here," I said. "I might need to borrow it."

The aide smiled. "Oh, you're new here," he said. "The typewriters are in the business room in the east wing. There are classes in there all day. The room is locked at night, but I'm sure you have a key."

I thanked him, and he turned his attention to a young man who was looking for a book about auto repair. On my way back to the guard office, I ran into Frank Hudson. Since he was alone, I decided to try to get him to talk some more about Ben Jones.

"Hey, Frank," I said. "Rumor has it

that Ernie will be getting out of here soon. He always said he was innocent. His lawyer must have found proof that someone else killed Jones."

"I heard that, too," Frank said evenly. Nothing seemed to fluster this man. "I'll believe it when I see it."

"Do you think Ernie is guilty?" I asked him.

"It doesn't matter what I think," Frank replied. "A judge and a jury sent him here. That's the bottom line. The way the system works, as long as someone pays for the crime, everybody's happy. Guilty or innocent, it doesn't matter."

"Is that really the way you feel?" I asked him. "Or is that just the way you think things are because you're in here now?"

"Hey, it didn't matter that Jones was the one who cooked up our whole plan," Frank said. "Once he was dead, they just had to find someone else to punish. So they picked me. I had nothing to do with most of the stuff he pulled. But they were determined to make someone pay."

"They?" I asked.

"Sure," he replied, "Police, judges, even prison guards. They want the appearance of justice. The real thing doesn't interest them."

Now Frank had my attention. I was thinking of him less as a possible murder suspect and more as an informant. I didn't believe he was as innocent as he claimed, but he did have an interesting view of life at Stanton Prison.

"Let me ask you a question, Frank. I don't know much about how things work around here," I said. "But let's say a prisoner wanted to send a note to another prisoner in the middle of the night. The prisoners are locked in different cells. How would he deliver the note?"

Frank laughed out loud. "That's easy," he said. "He would get a guard to do it." Frank was still laughing as he walked toward the library.

Chapter 12

Harry came through for me again. He got a clean set of prints off Ernie's note. And it didn't take him long to match those prints to the man who killed Ben Jones.

I'd already eliminated Rhonda Hudson and Lee Ruiz from my list of suspects. It didn't seem likely that they could hit Jones hard enough to kill him with just one blow. The piece of driftwood I had found wasn't very heavy, so the killer had to be strong. By the time that piece of driftwood floated back to shore, there were no fingerprints or bloodstains left on it. But the lab did find one tiny piece of hair embedded in the wood. The hair belonged to Ben Jones.

The coroner agreed that the size and shape of the driftwood was consistent with Jones' injury. We didn't have any fingerprints to connect the murderer to the weapon. But Ted Hayes had enough evidence to convince a judge to reexamine Ernie's conviction.

I was still hoping for a confession. That would complete our case against Jason Brown. I wanted to hear him explain why he killed Ben Jones. I've spoken to a lot of killers, and their motives always surprise me.

Harry brought Jason in for questioning. I listened in from the room next door. He told Jason that his fingerprints were on the note threatening Ernie. Harry also told him that we had the murder weapon.

But Jason still didn't crack. He told Harry that he delivered the note for someone else. And he said he didn't know anything about the murder or the murder weapon. Harry left Jason in the room and came to talk to me.

"I don't know what to do, Tony," Harry said. "He's just not rolling over. I know he did it, but I need his confession. The evidence we have isn't any stronger than what we had on Ernie."

"I know, Harry," I said. "But I'm sure Jason is the killer. I've been thinking. I checked out that business room where Jason typed the threatening notes. All the classroom doors were recently fitted with keyless locks. Jason had to swipe a card to get in. And a computer keeps track of who goes in at what time."

I could see that Harry was already thinking about what to say to Jason next.

"I spoke to the warden," I went on, "and the activity printouts are not running yet for those doors. But Jason probably doesn't know that. What if we tell him that we can prove that he was in that room, after lights-out, on both nights that Ernie received threats?"

"Let's go get him!" Harry said. "Come with me."

When I walked into the interrogation room, Jason looked surprised to see me. He still thought I was a prison guard from another town.

"I was sent to Stanton Prison under cover," I said, "to find out who was threatening Ernie Clement. And I have proof that it was you."

"Tony brought me printouts from the new lock on the business-room door," Harry said. "We know it was you who wrote and delivered the notes. Maybe you should just tell us your story now and hope for the best."

Jason looked a little scared. "What are you saying?" he asked. "Are you telling me that I'll get off easy if I confess?"

"That's between you and the district attorney," Harry said.

"I want a lawyer," Jason pleaded. "I need to make a phone call."

I looked over at Harry and smiled. We finally had the killer.

After his lawyer arrived, Jason told us everything.

It turns out that Jason's life wasn't as rosy as most people believed. His wife was ready to take the kids and walk out on him. Jason had signed a two-year lease, and she couldn't stand living in that dump. So Jason was desperate to get the place fixed up and keep his family together.

Jason had been doing security for some political events downtown. He knew the mayor and a city-code enforcer. He arranged to meet Ben

Jones out by the creek. Then he tried to threaten him by mentioning some important names downtown.

But Jones wasn't scared. He turned around and walked away. Jason panicked. He saw the piece of driftwood and picked it up. He ran up behind Jones and smashed him on the back of his head.

Harry had everything under control, so I figured it was time for me to go.

"I couldn't have done this without your help in taking that stuff to the lab," I said.

"No trouble at all," Harry said. "We make a good team. It's just too bad it took so long to get to the truth."

"Ted's already working on Ernie's release," I said. "Soon we'll have Jason behind bars, where he belongs."

I shook Harry's hand and said goodbye. "I'll see you," I said, turning toward the door.

"Hey, Tony!" I heard Harry yell to me. "If you ever want to be a cop again, just let me know. I might be able to make room for you here."

I just chuckled and waved. All I could think of was picking up Chance and maybe dropping in to see what Mamaw had cooking.